For Tommy, Billy, Emma and Katie —J.D.

DIAL BOOKS FOR YOUNG READERS
A division of Penguin Young Readers Group
Published by The Penguin Group
Penguin Group (USA) Inc., 375 Hudson Street, New York, NY 10014, U.S.A.
Penguin Group (Canada), 90 Eglinton Avenue East, Suite 700, Toronto,
Ontario, Canada M4P 2Y3 (a division of Pearson Penguin Canada Inc.)
Penguin Books Ltd, 80 Strand, London WC2R 0RL, England
Penguin Ireland, 25 St. Stephen's Green, Dublin 2, Ireland (a division of Penguin Books Ltd)
Penguin Group (Australia), 250 Camberwell Road, Camberwell, Victoria 3124, Australia (a division of Pearson Australia Group Pty Ltd)
Penguin Books India Pvt Ltd, 11 Community Centre, Panchsheel Park, New Delhi - 110 017, India
Penguin Group (NZ), Cnr Airborne and Rosedale Roads, Albany, Auckland 1310, New Zealand (a division of Pearson New Zealand Ltd)
Penguin Books (South Africa) (Pty) Ltd, 24 Sturdee Avenue, Rosebank, Johannesburg 2196, South Africa
Penguin Books Ltd, Registered Offices: 80 Strand, London WC2R 0RL, England
First published in the United States 2008 by
Dial Books for Young Readers
Originally published as *Monkey Puzzle* in Great Britain 2000 by
Macmillan Children's Books
Text copyright © 2000 by Julia Donaldson
Pictures copyright © 2000 by Axel Scheffler
All rights reserved
The publisher does not have any control over and does not assume any
responsibility for author or third-party websites or their content.
Printed in Belgium
1 3 5 7 9 10 8 6 4 2
Library of Congress Cataloging-in-Publication Data
Donaldson, Julia.
[Monkey puzzle]
Where's my mom? / Julia Donaldson ; [illustrated by] Axel Scheffler.
p.   cm.
Summary: A butterfly tries to help a lost young monkey find its mother in the jungle, meeting many different animals along the way.
ISBN-13: 978-0-8037-3228-5
[1. Monkeys—Fiction. 2. Butterflies—Fiction. 3. Jungle animals—Fiction. 4. Stories in rhyme.] I. Scheffler, Axel, ill. II. Title. III. Title: Where is my mom?
PZ8.3.D7235 2008   [E]—dc22   2007005236

Julia Donaldson   Axel Scheffler

Where's My Mom?

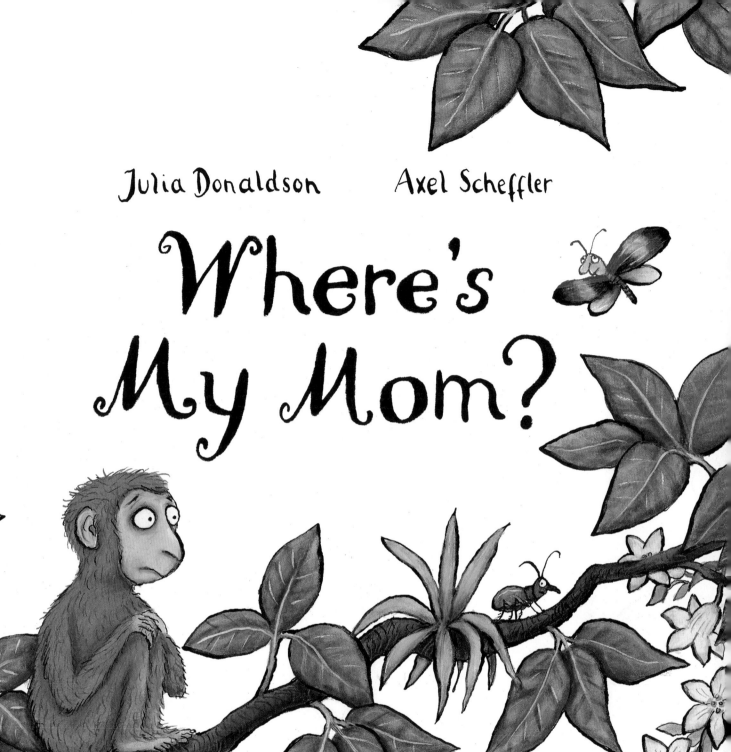

Dial Books for Young Readers

"I've lost my mom!"

"Hush, little monkey, don't you cry.
I'll help you find her," said butterfly.
"Let's have a think. How big is she?"

"She's big!" said the monkey. "Bigger than me."

"Bigger than you? Then I've seen your mom.
Come, little monkey, come, come, come."

"No, no, no! That's an elephant.

My mom isn't a great gray hunk.
She hasn't got tusks or a curly trunk.
She doesn't have great thick baggy knees.
And anyway, *her* tail coils round trees."

"She coils round trees? Then she's very near.
Quick, little monkey! She's over here."

"No, no, no! That's a snake.

Mom doesn't look a *bit* like this.
She doesn't slither about and hiss.
She doesn't curl round a nest of eggs.
And anyway, my mom's
got more legs."

"It's legs we're looking for now, you say?
I know where she is, then. Come this way."

"No, no, no! That's a spider.

Mom isn't black and hairy and fat.
She's not got so many legs as *that!*
She'd rather eat fruit than swallow a fly,
And she lives in the treetops, way up high."

"She lives in the trees? You should have said!

Your mommy's hiding above your head."

"No, no, no! That's a parrot.

Mom's got a nose and not a beak.

She doesn't squawk and squabble and shriek.

She doesn't have claws or feathery wings.

And anyway, my mom leaps and springs."

"Aha! I've got it! She leaps about?
She's just round the corner, without a doubt."

"No, no, no! That's a frog!

Butterfly, butterfly, please don't joke!
Mom's not green and she doesn't croak.
She's not all slimy. Oh, dear, what a muddle!
She's brown and furry, and nice to cuddle."

"Brown fur—why didn't you tell me so?
We'll find her in no time—off we go!"

"No, no, no! That's a bat.

Why do you keep on getting it wrong?
Mom doesn't sleep the whole day long.
I told you, she's got no wings at all,
And anyway, she's not *nearly* so small!"

"Your mom's not little? Now let me think.
She's down by the river, having a drink!"

"NO, NO, NO!
That's the elephant again!

"Butterfly, butterfly, can't you see?

None of these creatures look like me!"

"You never told me she looked like you!"

"Of course I didn't! I thought you knew!"

"I didn't know. I couldn't! You see . . .

" . . . None of my babies look like me.
So she looks like you! Well, if that's *the case*
We'll soon discover her hiding place."

"No, no, no! That's my dad!"

"Come, little monkey, come, come, come.

It's time I took you home to . . ."

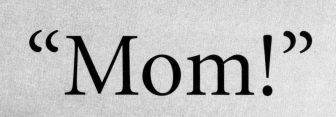

"Mom!"